D1642383

A catalogue record for this book is available from the British Library

Published by Ladybird Books Ltd
A subsidiary of the Penguin Group
A Pearson Company
LADYBIRD and the device of a Ladybird are trademarks of Ladybird Books Ltd Loughborough Leicestershire UK
© Disney MCMXCVII
Based on the book by Dodie Smith. Published by William Heinemann Limited.

All rights reserved. No part of this publication may be reproduced, stored in a retrieval system, or transmitted in any form or by any means, electronic, mechanical, photocopying, recording or otherwise, without the prior consent of the copyright owner.

Disney's

101 DALMATIANS

Ladybird

My name is Pongo. I'm a Dalmatian, and I've always lived in London with my owner, Roger Radcliff.

Roger is a musician, and there was a time when he spent every day alone at his piano, writing songs. Our life together was pleasant but much too dull – and one day I decided to do something about it. I saw a lovely woman and her Dalmatian walking to the park, so I got Roger to take me for a walk, too.

In the park, I managed to get Roger and the woman tangled up in my lead, which was very embarrassing for both of them. But they didn't stay embarrassed for long. When the lady, who was called Anita, and Roger looked in one another's eyes, their hearts melted.

Roger and Anita soon fell in love – which made me very happy as I was already in love with Perdita, Anita's beautiful Dalmatian.

That spring, Roger and Anita got married. Perdy and I were thrilled, because that meant we would be together, too. We all moved to a cosy house near the park. A kind, cheerful woman called Nanny came to be our cook and housekeeper.

A few months later, Perdy and I became the proud parents of fifteen adorable puppies. Our joy was complete, and Roger, Anita and Nanny were delighted.

Life seemed perfect – until the day our peace and happiness were shattered by a ring on the doorbell.

In walked a frightful-looking woman in an enormous fur coat. It was Cruella De Vil – someone Anita had known at school. Anita had never liked her. Still, she invited her in, just to be polite.

"I heard you had some Dalmatian puppies," Cruella said. "I simply *adore* Dalmatians – such lovely coats! I want to buy the puppies. Name your price – I'll take them all."

She took out her cheque book and fountain pen.

Roger, who despised Cruella, was furious. "The puppies aren't for sale," he said. "Not a single one is leaving this house. Do you understand?"

Cruella couldn't believe her ears. "Surely he must be joking!" she said to Anita.

But Roger was firm. "No, I mean it," he declared. "And that's final!"

Cruella flew into a rage. "All right, keep the little beasts!" she shrieked. "But I'll get even with you! You fools! You'll be sorry for this!"

She stormed out, slamming the door behind her.

The puppies grew so quickly and were so full of mischief that we had no time to think about Cruella. In a few weeks' time, we had forgotten all about her.

Then, one night while Perdy and I were out for our walk with Roger and Anita, two suspicious characters called Horace and Jasper forced their way into our house. Nanny tried her best to stop them, but they locked her in a cupboard.

By the time Nanny managed to free herself, it was too late. Horace and Jasper were gone, and so were all the puppies. When we arrived home, we found Nanny searching frantically up and down the street.

Nanny told us what had happened, and Roger and Anita phoned the police. They launched an investigation, but the dognappers hadn't left a single clue. Our puppies had disappeared without a trace.

Perdy and I knew there was only one thing to do – we would have to find our puppies ourselves. "We'll use the Twilight Bark," I told Perdy.

When Roger and Anita took us for our walk that evening, Perdy and I barked our message from a hilltop in the park: "Fifteen Dalmatian puppies stolen."

The message was heard and sent on by dogs all over the city. It finally made its way to a farm in the countryside, where it was picked up by an old sheepdog named the Colonel and his friend, a cat called Sergeant Tibs.

"I heard puppies barking at the old De Vil mansion," said Sergeant Tibs. "Let's go and have a look."

The Colonel and Tibs made their way to the gloomy old house and peered through a window. They could see some puppies, so Tibs crawled through a hole in the wall to get a better look.

He was amazed at what he found – not just fifteen, but *ninety-nine* Dalmatian puppies!

"We're not all stolen," one of the puppies told Sergeant Tibs. "Some of us came from pet shops."

He went on to warn Tibs about the Baduns – Horace and Jasper, who were sprawled on the settee, watching television.

A moment later, Cruella De Vil burst in.

"Get up, you idiots!" she shouted at Horace and Jasper. "I want the skins of those puppies to make fur coats, and I want them tonight! Get to work, or there'll be big trouble!" She hurled a bottle into the fireplace and slammed out of the room.

Sergeant Tibs was horrified. He had to get the puppies out of there right away!

"Hey, kids," he whispered, "come with me!"

Quickly and quietly, Tibs led the puppies through the hole in the wall and out into the hallway. But they hadn't got far when the Baduns stopped them.

"Trying to run out on us, eh?" said Jasper. "Double-crossing little brutes!" He and Horace locked the puppies in a room under the stairs.

Meanwhile, the Twilight Bark had let Perdy and me know that our puppies had been found. We set out at once, trudging across icy fields and through freezing streams, hoping we weren't too late.

When we got to the house, we saw Horace and Jasper standing over the puppies. Jasper was threatening them with a fire poker. Growling and snarling, we crashed through a window and attacked.

Perdy tore at Jasper's trouser leg, and I lunged at him. Jasper turned in fury, then rushed at me with the poker. I slipped between his legs and escaped.

I snapped at Jasper and knocked him down, while Perdy went for Horace. He stumbled right into the fireplace. "Help! Fire!" he cried, staggering around blindly. He crashed into Jasper, and the two landed in a helpless heap against the wall.

After making sure our fifteen puppies were there, Perdy and I led all ninety-nine out into the snow. We'd heard what Cruella planned to do with them, so we knew we had to take them all home to Roger and Anita.

Sergeant Tibs told us about a farm where we would be safe for a while, and we set out. We made sure to cover our tracks so Horace and Jasper couldn't follow us.

It was a long way to the farm. When we finally got there the puppies were shivering and exhausted.

We took shelter in the barn, where the cows made us very welcome – and gave the puppies as much fresh, warm milk as they could drink.

As Perdy and I thanked the cows, the kind collie who lived on the farm shared some scraps of meat with us.

"I know a Labrador in a village near here who might be able to help you," he told us. "Get some rest, because you'll need to make an early start tomorrow."

The Labrador was waiting when we arrived at the village, and he took us to an abandoned blacksmith's shop. From the window, we could see a furniture lorry that was going to London. "There'll be room for all of you," the Labrador assured us.

Suddenly Perdy began to tremble. "Pongo, look!" she cried. Cruella De Vil was driving towards the shop! And Horace and Jasper were in a van right behind her.

We had to find a way to get to the lorry without being seen. So we took it in turns to roll in some piles of soot, and soon we all looked like Labradors!

Cruella stared as we carried the puppies into the lorry, but she didn't say a word – until some melting snow fell on a few of the puppies and washed away the soot. "It's the Dalmatians!" she shouted to Horace and Jasper. "After them!"

Luckily, we had all made it safely into the lorry by the time the chase began. Cruella tried to force the lorry off the road, but her car skidded and hurtled downhill into a snowdrift. The Baduns' van went crashing into her car, and they all ended up together in a pile of wreckage. We knew that would be the last we saw of Cruella and her friends, so we all settled down to enjoy the journey.

Later that day, we finally arrived in London. We were tired and dirty, but very happy to be safe at home again with the people we loved.

Roger, Anita and Nanny could hardly believe their eyes. They were overjoyed, and they fell in love with all ninety-nine puppies.

"We'll keep them all!" Roger said, laughing happily. "We'll buy a big house in the country and have a Dalmatian Plantation!"

Roger was so inspired by his idea that he rushed to the piano to begin composing a new song. As he pounded away at the keys, we all barked along with the music. Soon the whole house resounded with joyful voices – the voices of one hundred and one Dalmatians.